The Magic Melon

A Chinese fairy tale

Retold by
Rosie Dickins

Illustrated by Sara Rojo

Reading consultant: Alison Kelly
Roehampton University

This story
is about
lazy Lee,

a kind
old man,

a magic melon

and a magic melon seed.

3

Lee hated working.

He liked snoozing
much better.

6

8

Soon, Lee was very hungry.

Then he saw an old
man with a melon.

"This is a magic melon,"
said the man.

"What do you want for dinner?"

"Fried rice," sighed Lee.

The man tapped
the melon.

Tap tap tap

Ping! There was a bowl
of tasty rice.

13

Lee ate and ate. "I wish *I* had a magic melon!"

"You can grow one," said the man. "But it's hard work!"

"Here is a seed. Plant it
carefully."

"You must water it three times a day."

At first, Lee did as he
was told.

But not for long...

Zzzzz

The melon grew bigger...

and bigger.

One day, Lee picked it.

He licked his lips and wished for dinner.

Someone laughed.
It was the old man.

You didn't
look after it,
did you?

Designed by Caroline Spatz
Series designer: Russell Punter
Series editor: Lesley Sims

First published in 2012 by Usborne Publishing Ltd., Usborne House,
83-85 Saffron Hill, London EC1N 8RT, England. www.usborne.com
Copyright © 2012 Usborne Publishing Ltd.

Puzzle 3

birds

hat

bowls

melon

bread

bucket

About the story

The Magic Melon is a very old
Chinese tale. It has been retold
many times. In some versions, the
magic fruit is a kind of pumpkin
known as a gourd.

Answers to puzzles

Puzzle 1

Puzzle 2

B   D   A   C

Puzzle 3

Find these things in the picture:

bowls   hat   birds

bread   bucket   melon

Puzzle 2

Look at the pictures and put them in order:

A

B

C

D

There are six to find.

PUZZLES

Puzzle 1

Can you spot the differences between these two pictures?

"You cheated the melon,"
he said.

"Now the melon is
cheating you!"